W9-AHW-575

How the CAT Swallowed Thunder

by
LLOYD ALEXANDER

illustrated by
Judith Byron Schachner

PUFFIN BOOKS

For all my thunderers—L.A.
To Lisa—J.B.S.

PUFFIN BOOKS
Published by the Penguin Group
Penguin Putnam Books for Young Readers,
345 Hudson Street, New York, New York 10014, U.S.A.
Penguin Books Ltd, 80 Strand, London WC2R ORL, England
Penguin Books Australia Ltd, 250 Camberwell Road, Camberwell, Victoria 3124, Australia
Penguin Books Canada Ltd, 10 Alcorn Avenue, Toronto, Ontario, Canada M4V 3B2
Penguin Books (N.Z.) Ltd, 182-190 Wairau Road, Auckland 10, New Zealand

Penguin Books Ltd, Registered Offices: Harmondsworth, Middlesex, England

First published in the United States of America by Dutton Children's Books,
a division of Penguin Putnam Books for Young Readers, 2000
Published by Puffin Books, a division of Penguin Putnam Books for Young Readers, 2003

1 3 5 7 9 10 8 6 4 2

Text copyright © Lloyd Alexander, 2000
Illustrations copyright © Judith Byron Schachner, 2000
All rights reserved

THE LIBRARY OF CONGRESS HAS CATALOGED THE DUTTON EDITION AS FOLLOWS:
Alexander, Lloyd.
How the cat swallowed thunder / by Lloyd Alexander;
illustrated by Judith Byron Schachner—1st ed.   p.   cm.
Summary: Warned not to get into his usual mischief, Mother Holly's cat
tries to tidy up all the mess he has made while she is away.
ISBN: 0-525-46449-2 (hc)
[1. Cats—Fiction. 2. Behavior—Fiction.] I. Schachner, Judith Byron, ill. II. Title.
PZ7.A3774 Hr 2000 [E]—dc21 00-024530

Puffin Books ISBN 0-14-250003-8

Manufactured in China

Except in the United States of America, this book is sold subject to the condition that
it shall not, by way of trade or otherwise, be lent, re-sold, hired out, or otherwise
circulated without the publisher's prior consent in any form of binding or cover
other than that in which it is published and without a similar condition
including this condition being imposed on the subsequent purchaser.

There was a time when the Cat had no purr. In those days, he lived with old Mother Holly in her cottage. Quick with his paws, he would pounce on her spinning wheel and tangle himself in the thread, upset the churn and lick the butter, climb into the cupboard and dance after his tail amid the crockery. Such a rascal was he that Mother Holly never let him out of her sight, for fear his next scrape would be worse than his last.

One morning, however, after she had put on her apron and tied a kerchief about her head, she called the Cat and told him:

"Cat, of all my creatures in this world, there's none like you for setting things topsy-turvy. But now it's time you learned to behave and to make yourself useful.

"I have errands to do: a cooing lesson for my doves; fresh honey-suckle for my bees; and a leaky brook to mend. While I'm gone, I want you to make the bed, sweep the floor, stir the soup, and tidy up the cottage. And, when I come back, if I find even one thing amiss—then, believe me, it will be so much the worse for you."

The Cat promised to do all these tasks, and Mother Holly set off on her errands.

The Cat fetched the broom from the corner, but after a minute's worth of sweeping he stopped and shook his head.

"This business of housekeeping," he said to himself, "it's weary work so early in the day."

And he began to eye the plump goose-feather pillows and soft eiderdown quilt on Mother Holly's bed.

"A morning nap would be strengthening," he said. "I'll work much harder once I've had forty winks, or even eighty. So, no need to sweep the floor until I've made the bed. And no need to make the bed until I've had my nap in it."

Then he remembered Mother Holly's telling him to stir the soup, and it also occurred to him that he was hungry.

"I'll sleep more soundly on a full stomach," said the Cat, "and the better I sleep, the better I'll sweep. And, of course, I'll have to taste that soup to make sure it's properly stirred.

"So, first things first," declared the Cat, and he dropped the broom and hurried to the stove. The iron kettle simmered so merrily and so temptingly that he could not wait another moment.

"The best is always at the bottom," said the Cat, taking a long wooden spoon and stirring vigorously until the tastiest morsels came bobbing up. However, the soup smelled so delicious, and he was so eager for a taste that he forgot to blow on it. As the hot broth burned his tongue, he flung away the spoon, and some of the soup spattered onto the floor.

"If Mother Holly sees that spot," he groaned, "I'm in a pickle for sure."

He rummaged about the kitchen until he found a scrubbing brush and began scrubbing away as hard as he could. But this only made the spot worse.

"If it won't scrub out," said the Cat, "then it will have to wash out. Water—that's what I need."

His eye fell on a battered watering can standing in the corner.
"Just the thing," said the Cat. "A little sprinkle here, a little sprinkle there, and that will set everything right."

No sooner did he begin, however, than he felt raindrops pattering on his head.

"Is Mother Holly's roof leaking?" he wondered, glancing up. Yet, as he saw through the window, the sky was a cloudless blue, with not a sign of rain. So he shrugged and went back to his work.

But the more he sprinkled, the more it showered, until a whole cloudburst was pelting down. His fur was drenched, his whiskers dripping, and the kitchen was everywhere awash with puddles.

"What kind of watering can is this?" cried the Cat. "I sprinkle the floor and along comes a rainstorm! Oh, if Mother Holly comes back and finds her kitchen a duck pond...!"

The besodden Cat seized a mop hanging behind the door and plied it desperately. By the time he had finished swabbing and wringing, wringing and swabbing, he was puffing from his efforts. The floor, at last, was clean and spotless.

But he noticed a sack of corn had been soaked by the downpour.

"Ah, that won't do at all," said the Cat. "If Mother Holly sees her corn is wet..."

So he put the sack on the hearth where the fire could warm it. However, the embers had died down, and the heat they gave was hardly enough to dry the grain. Furthermore, the Cat was feeling chilly after his drenching.

"The fire needs more wood," said the Cat, setting a log on the andirons. "This should build it up a little. That way, the corn and I will both be well toasted."

As the log was slow to burn, the Cat picked up a pair of bellows from the chimney corner and started pumping away. But no sooner did the air come whistling out of the bellows than a cold breeze began stirring through the cottage.

"There's a nasty draft in here," the Cat remarked, continuing to work the bellows. But the harder he pumped, the harder the breeze blew, until soon it was howling around his ears. Alarmed, he threw down the bellows, and the wind immediately stopped.

"What kind of bellows are these?" cried the Cat. "The cottage had a good airing—there's not a speck of dust to be seen. But it's lucky the roof didn't go sailing off!"

"That's what comes of working before resting," he told himself. "I should never have put off taking my nap. Now I'll have to sleep twice as soundly to make up for it."

So he hopped into the bed, tugged and pummeled the pillow to suit his comfort, hooked his claws into the quilt, and rolled himself up in it. He tucked his paws under his chin and soon was happily drowsing.

Meantime, the fire blazed higher and higher, so hot that the corn swelled and stirred and spilled out of the sack.

While the Cat snored away peacefully, the corn grew hotter. And the hotter it grew, the more it swelled, until one kernel split its hull, then another and another—flying from the top of the sack. As the corn burst, violent peals of thunder shook the cottage.

Jolted out of his slumber, the Cat tore loose from the bedclothes, fur bristling, yowling in fright. He dove under Mother Holly's rug, certain the cottage was tumbling about his head. The windows rattled, cups and saucers jiggled on the shelf, and the floor trembled beneath his paws.

Realizing the bursting corn was causing the thunderbolts, the Cat plucked up all his courage, darted to the fireplace, and snatched away the sack before the rest of the kernels exploded.

"What kind of corn is this?" cried the Cat, whiskers twitching and ears ringing. "Good thing there's no harm done with all that boom and bluster. But it's ruined my nap, and that's damage enough."

He turned to climb back into the bed but stopped in his tracks, rubbed his eyes, and miauled in dismay. The cottage was rapidly filling with snow.

Goose feathers were streaming from the bed, floating upward like a cloud of dandelion puffs. As they did, snowflakes whirled in the air and settled over the table, the chair, the spinning wheel, and the butter churn.

Waving his paws, the Cat plunged through the white flakes and went slipping and sliding to the bed. The feathers, he saw, poured from the quilt and pillow where his claws had ripped them. He snatched at the feathers and in vain tried to stuff them back.

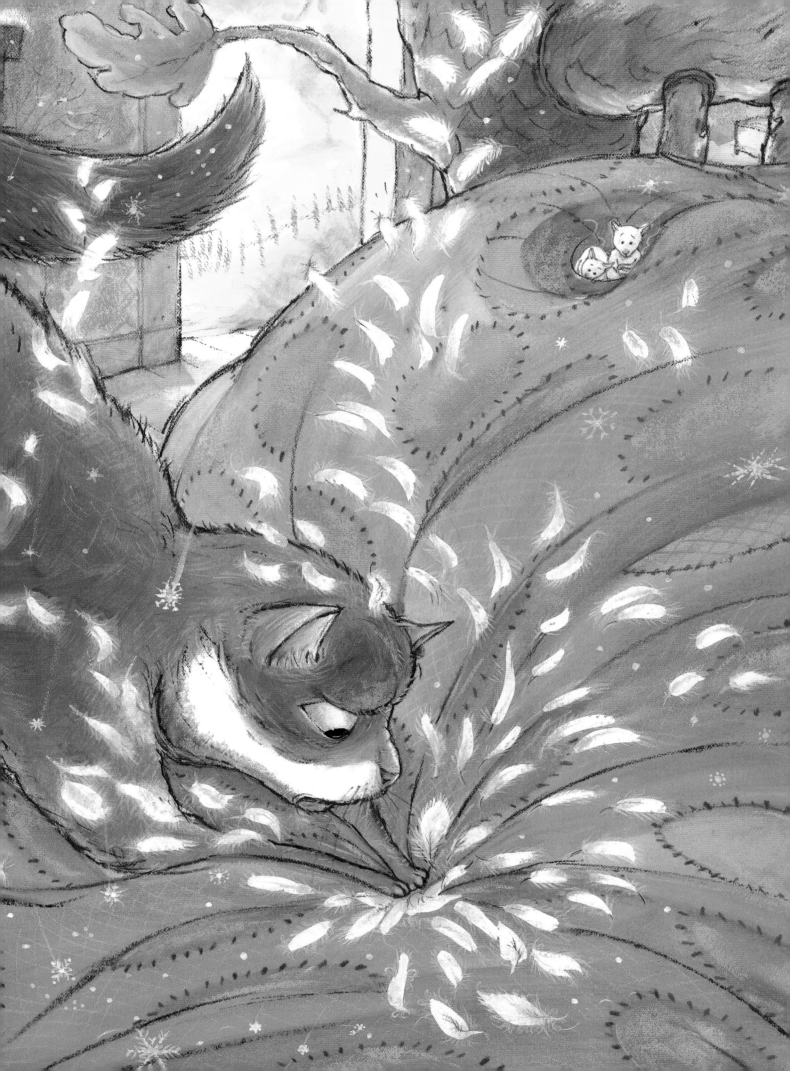

Seeing his only hope lay in smothering the spate of goose feathers, he hastily spread the linen coverlet over the bed, smoothed it down, and tucked in the corners. By the time he had finished, the bed was made as neatly as Mother Holly herself would have done. The snowfall stopped, but the Cat held his head at the sight of the drifts.

"A goose-feather blizzard!" he wailed. "If Mother Holly sees that...!"

He seized the broom and, as fast as he could, swept the snow out the door, where it quickly melted. Then, with his tail, he dusted the remaining flakes from every stick of furniture and, for good measure, polished the crockery.

Scarcely had he finished when he heard Mother Holly's footsteps coming up the path. That same instant, he glimpsed a tiny fragment of corn lying in the middle of the kitchen floor.

"Mother Holly warned me!" cried the Cat. "The least thing amiss..."

He pounced on the corn just as Mother Holly opened the door and stepped across the sill.

With no time to hide the broken kernel, and not daring to throw it into the fire, the Cat popped it into his mouth.

Then he hurried to sit in the corner, curled his tail around him, and smiled as blandly as if he had never a care in the world.

Putting down her basket, Mother Holly turned a searching glance from the neatly made bed to the gleaming, well-scrubbed floor. She looked into the soup kettle, peered under the bed, and ran her finger over the cupboard shelves.

"My dear Cat," she exclaimed, beaming. "You've done wonders here! I've never seen my cottage so tidy! And to think I took you for a rascal. But what a fine, industrious Cat you are!"

"Umm-mm," answered the Cat, trying to keep the corn from falling out of his mouth.

"No need for such modesty," said Mother Holly. "You should be proud of yourself. And you've earned a reward. You'll have a bowl of lovely warm cream and a supper of everything you like best; then I'll let you sleep on my goose-feather pillow as long as you want. What do you say to that?"

The Cat, never opening his lips, eagerly bobbed his head.

"Come, come," said Mother Holly. "It's bad manners, nodding when you're asked a question. You must learn to be polite and say, 'Thank you.'"

"Mmf-mmu," mumbled the Cat.

"You, at a loss for words?" Mother Holly eyed the Cat sharply. "Are you eating something? What's in your mouth? Here, let me see."

"It's—it's nothing," stammered the Cat, gulping down the fragment.

An instant later, his eyes widened and he clapped his paws to his belly, for the kernel had begun buzzing and rumbling.

"Whatever's the matter with you?" demanded Mother Holly as the Cat yawned, gaped, jigged up and down, and even stood on his head, trying every way to disgorge the corn.

"Help! Help!" he gasped. "I swallowed a piece of thunder!"

"Don't be silly," replied Mother Holly. "You couldn't have done that. Not unless you ate some corn from my sack."

"Yes, I did!" wailed the Cat. "I didn't mean to! It's no fault of mine. The watering can started it—"

"What?" cried Mother Holly. "Are you telling me you've been at my watering can? The one I use for my April showers?"

"Yes, but I mopped up the flood," pleaded the Cat. "It was the bellows made the fire too hot—"

"Flood?" cried Mother Holly. "Bellows, too? My March winds! As soon as I let you out of my sight—"

"But I swept out the snow," protested the Cat. "I mean, the goose feathers."

He blurted out all that had happened, then shrank back on his haunches, waiting to hear either a blast of thunder or Mother Holly pronounce his punishment, whichever came first.

"You know what I told you," said Mother Holly, frowning and shaking a finger at him. "So much the worse for you...."

Then she stopped and cupped her ear.

"Cat, what noise are you making?"

"Not me," groaned the Cat. "It's that thunder about to explode, and me along with it."

"Nonsense," Mother Holly said. "There's not enough thunder in that little broken bit of corn to harm a flea. And it's nothing to what you deserve for your mischief."

She stopped again and listened.

"But what a curious sound that is. Rather like my bees gathering nectar on a summer afternoon."

"Bees!" cried the Cat. "I'm to live in a hive!" And he tried his best to stifle the noise.

"No, it's more like my doves," Mother Holly said, her face lightening, "cooing together in their nest."

"Pigeons!" moaned the Cat. "She's going to put me up in a tree!" And he tried all the harder to choke off the rumbling.

"I do believe it's more like my brook," said Mother Holly, "bubbling over mossy stones."

"She means to have me paddling with the ducks!" wailed the Cat, able at last to stop and start the buzzing as he chose. "Mother Holly, I promise I'll never make that noise again!"

Instead of a frown, a smile now spread over Mother Holly's face.

"Do keep on," she urged. "My dear Cat, what a marvelous song! How strange—it makes me feel so happy and peaceful."

"Indeed?" answered the Cat, his spirits beginning to lift. "And you'd like more?"

"Oh, yes!" Mother Holly clapped her hands and beamed in delight. "I've never heard anything quite like it. So lovely, so charming—"

"Ah yes, well," replied the Cat, thinking quickly, "there's one small difficulty. It's very tiring. And it does seem to sharpen my appetite. Ah…that cream you spoke about, and the nap…"

"You'll have all I promised," said Mother Holly, picking up the Cat and setting him on her lap, "if only you'll sing for me again."

"Gladly," said the Cat. "Though, naturally, a little combing and brushing would keep me in better voice."

"You'll be combed and brushed every day," Mother Holly assured him. "And stroked and patted to your heart's content."

"In that case, there's nothing more I could ask," replied the Cat. "At least, not for the moment."

And he began to sing again, so gently and soothingly that he sang Mother Holly to sleep—and, before long, himself as well.

Edison Twp. Free Pub. Library
North Edison Branch
777 Grove Ave.
Edison, NJ 08820

EDISON TWP. FREE PUBLIC LIBRARY
3 9360 00528382 8

Edison Twp. Free Pub. Library
North Edison Branch
777 Grove Ave.
Edison, NJ 08820